chronicle books san francisco

Construction Site on Christmas Night

IT'S ALMOST CHRISTMAS!

SHERRI DUSKEY RINKER AND AG FORD

Down in the big construction site,
there's work to do for Christmas night!

The last big project of the year;
the team is slamming into gear.

So much is riding on the crew—
they have a major job to do!

A special house is being built.
The trucks are racing at full tilt.

This important work can't wait;
they'll get it done and make it great.

Bulldozer's deadline is almost here.
He has a lot of ground to clear!

Working at full-speed all day (*rooaaar!*),
he pushes hard to clear the way.

For hours he powers, this way and that,
and clears the site in no time flat.

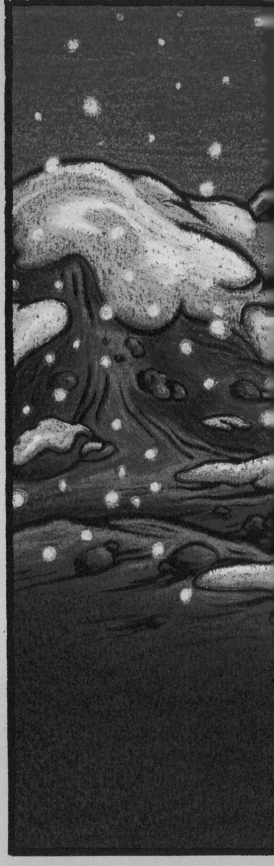

He turns away to end his shift,
but in his way: a MASSIVE gift!

With cable "ribbon" from the yard,
it's topped off with a thank-you card.

An awesome carbon steel blade—
custom paint job, custom made!

Merry Christmas, Bulldozer. Goodnight.

Excavator has no time to spare.
He's rolling, digging everywhere.

Scooping, chugging at
full blast (*vvvvvvrrr!*),

he digs up the foundation—fast!

Clouds roll in, a brisk wind blows,
a snowflake falls right on his nose!

The clock in town begins to chime.
His job's done right, and right on time.

As Excavator rolls away,
slowing down to end his day,

he stops—and can't believe his eyes.
Someone's left a BIG surprise:

the card says, "Thanks for all you do!"
and it's signed simply, "From our crew."

Look! A shiny yellow scoop!
(His old one has a broken tooth.)

Merry Christmas, Excavator. Goodnight.

THANKS
FOR ALL
YOU DO!
—FROM OUR CREW—

Cement Mixer has concrete to pour:
he lays the foundation, walls, and floor.

And then he churns
another load
that will be used
to make a road.

He twirls, he rolls, he spins, he pours.
In record time, he's done his chores.

He rolls away to take a bath,
but something's sitting in his path:

a GIANT box, his name's on top,
he rumbles to a grinding stop (*scrreeecchh!*).

No card, no note. Who is it from?
Who could have left . . .
a brand-new drum?!

His drum is old, beat up, and plain,
but this one's like a candy cane!

Merry Christmas, Cement Mixer. Goodnight.

An icy wind blows in his face,
but Dump Truck revs to keep the pace.

His back is sore, his tires are shot,
but Dump Truck gives it all he's got . . .

and soon, there's nothing left to haul.
He slows his engine to a crawl.

He turns to go, but stops in awe:
the BIGGEST box he ever saw!

He blows his stack, his engine fires (*vroom! vroom!*) . . .
it's a fresh new set of tires!

Midnight black with thick, tough tread.
He tucks the old ones in his bed.

Merry Christmas, Dump Truck. Goodnight.

With whipping winds and loads that sway
(*wooosshhh!*),
Crane Truck's job is tough today!

But he keeps working right along,
bravely lifting—firm and strong.

It's getting darker with each pass,
but Crane Truck's work is done at last.

The job's all finished. One last stop—
Crane Truck puts a star on top.

But Crane has one last thing to lift,
someone's left a SPECIAL gift:

a rock-'em-sock-'em wrecking ball!
It's red and green and ten feet tall.

Merry Christmas, Crane Truck. Goodnight.

Engines rev and bells ring out (*cling! cling!*),
sirens blare and air horns shout
(*rooooooooo! hooonnk!*).

Down the road and up the drive,
a fleet of bright-red trucks arrive.

Driving proudly, looking fine,
pumpers, ladders all in line.

Cars and rescue trucks join, too,
bright and shiny, rolling through . . .
it's the town's new FIRE CREW!

On this nearly Christmas night,
they find a new home, built just right.

And with a joyful roll and spin,
the fire trucks move right on in,

turn off ignitions, settle down,
and look out at the sleepy town . . .

All grateful for this special day,
and helpful friends at work and play,
for all that's given and received,
and all that's blessed this Christmas Eve . . .

Shhh. All the trucks are tucked in tight.
Merry Christmas! And . . . *goodnight.*

For Kelley, Jackie, and Ann—my oldest, dearest friends.
And for Jules, who patiently answered all my questions
about what trucks might want for Christmas —SDR

Text copyright © 2018 by Sherri Duskey Rinker.
Illustrations copyright © 2018 by AG Ford.
Artwork based on illustrations copyright © 2011–2017 by Tom Lichtenheld.

Library of Congress Cataloging-in-Publication Data:
Names: Rinker, Sherri Duskey, author. | Ford, AG, illustrator.
Title: Construction site on Christmas night / Sherri Duskey Rinker and AG Ford
Description: San Francisco, California : Chronicle Books LLC, [2018] |
Summary: It is Christmas Eve, and all the construction vehicles are
finishing up work on the site, and when they leave they find that there is a special present
waiting for each of them.
Identifiers: LCCN 2017060502 | ISBN 9781452139111 (alk. paper)
Subjects: LCSH: Construction equipment—Juvenile fiction. | Gifts—Juvenile fiction. | Christ-
mas stories. | Stories in rhyme. | CYAC: Stories in rhyme. | Construction equipment—Fiction.
| Gifts—Fiction. |
Christmas—Fiction. | LCGFT: Stories in rhyme.
Classification: LCC PZ8.3.R48123 Co 2018 | DDC [E]—
dc23 LC record available at https://lccn.loc.gov/2017060502

Manufactured in the United States of America.

Design by Kristine Brogno and Jill Turney
Typeset in Mr. Eaves.
The illustrations in this book were rendered in Neocolor wax oil crayons.

10 9 8 7 6 5 4 3
Chronicle Books LLC
680 Second Street
San Francisco, California 94107

Chronicle Books—we see things differently.
Become part of our community at www.chroniclekids.com.